Norman PhartEphant®

First New Day

Angela Larson
Illustrated by Kenny Durkin

A PUBLICATION BY FIERCE FUN TOYS, LLC.

This is a work of fiction. Names, characters, places and incidents either are the product of the author's imagination or are used fictitiously. Any resemblance to actual persons, living or dead, events or locals is entirely coincidental.

www.FierceFunToys.com

ISBN 978-1-61623-643-4

Manufactured in Shen Zhen, Guang Dong, P.R China, in 06/2010 by Printplus Limited

First Edition; Flex-Bound; 2010

Written by Angela Larson
Illustration by Kenny Durkin
Design/Layout by Tressa Foster
Edited by Lauren Vogelbaum

To: Zander & Tyler

Hello, I'm Norman,

Norman PhartEphant.

I'm an African elephant who
was adopted by this US zoo.
Alfrebit was alone, but now I'm
here, and we are a family of two.

Since coming to the zoo my diet
has changed and now... I fart.

I fart a lot.

You might think it is fun to fart,
but when you fart all the time,
it is not.

If I was alone, farting might not bother me— well, other than the smell. The thing is, I'm not alone. I don't want to be alone— I'm with Alfrebit.

Even if Alfrebit stands quietly in the corner pretending to sleep, I know he is listening, watching, and waiting... waiting for something interesting to happen.

With Alfrebit's great ears, he must hear me fart. But even if he misses the sound, he can catch the stink.

This zoo is new to me: the sights, the sounds, the smells, the other animals, and most of all...the food.

Everything is different than in Africa.
Not better and not worse, just different.

So here's the thing about farting: when a fart leaves my body, I'm in for a surprise.

Will it **stink?**

It is amazing that my body can be an instrument and make such sounds. It is amazing that the mix of gasses in my tummy can create such a symphony. The real surprise is in the timing. Farts sneak up on me, when I least expect them.

When I first came to the zoo,
I found it a bit scary.
I didn't know anyone. I was
even afraid of Alfrebit.

But as I looked around, I became
curious about what I saw.

Next door was a collection of
animals of brilliant colors like
butterflies, but with teeth and
claws like lions, and as sinister
and silent as panthers.

I had never seen anything
like them before.

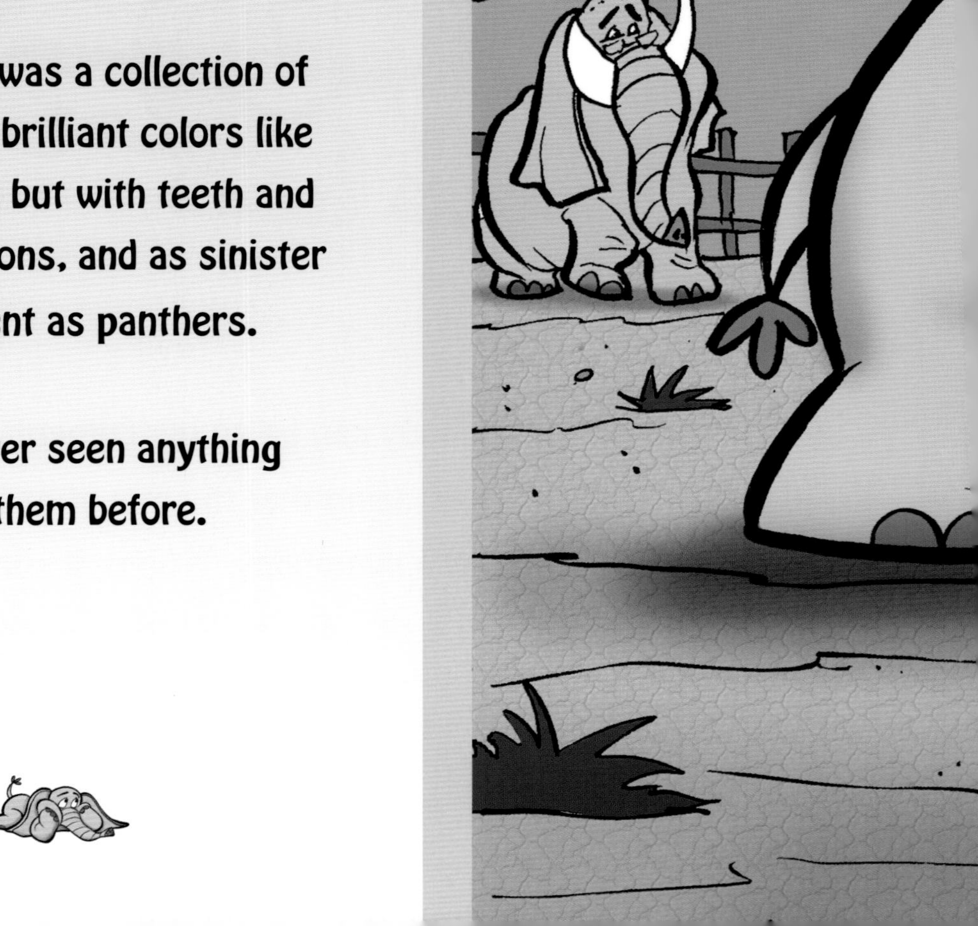

One day, one of the smaller crea-
tures was dozing by the fence,
soaking in the rays of the sun.

I snuck close to examine its fur of
orange and black stripes.

When I was near, I could see
that each hair was either orange
or black, not striped.

All of a sudden, one eye opened looking at me.
Then the other.

The eyebrows began to fold and the top lip rose.

With teeth bared, the animal made a low rumble
which rose into a growl.

I became scared. I wanted to back away.
I wanted to be invisible.

And just in that moment...

PHHHAAAT

"Excuse me," I said quickly to the creature now smiling before me.

As she sat up, the growl disappeared and the bared teeth began to look friendly.

She said, "I've never heard such a loud fart before. I guess you elephants with your greater size can make a bigger sound than us tigers."

"**You fart too?**" I asked.

"Yes" she replied, "but I try not to around others. Tigers have an image to protect. We try to look intimidating."

I introduced myself. "Hello, I'm Norman."

"Well hello, Norman. I'm Ty," she responded.

The rest of the day Ty and I chatted about what elephants and tigers had in common; we both love being outside, fresh air, and fresh food.

But I was amazed by our differences:
Ty is from India, whereas I'm from Africa.

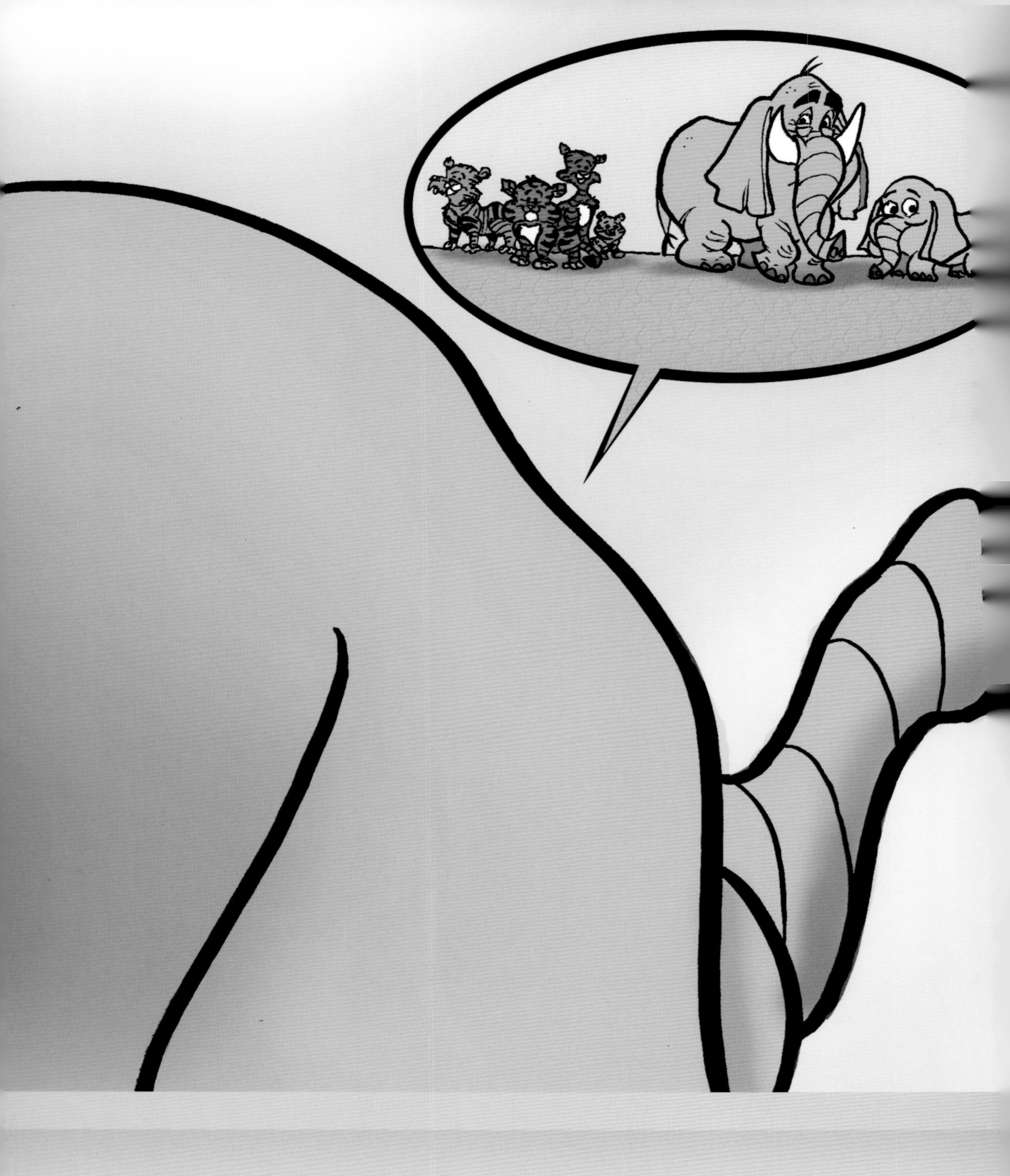

Ty has brothers and sisters and lives in a pride (a large family) whereas I live with Alfrebit (just the two of us).

Ty lives mostly in the jungle, eats meat, and is an expert tree climber. I can walk for miles through woods, forest and plains, I prefer to eat vegetables, and I can knock over trees, but not climb them.

That evening, I shared with Alfrebit what I had learned about Ty and India.

Alfrebit smiled at me and said, "Congratulation on the new friend, my little gassy machine. Tomorrow you must meet Zip. He's from Australia."

I went to sleep
excited about tomorrow.

About Fierce Fun Toys, LLC

(www.FierceFunToys.com)

Fierce Fun Toys started one fateful morning when its president, a mother of two boys, was struck with a thought during her morning shower, "This can't be all there is! I'm starting my own company!" Between her business acumen and her husband's flatulence proclivity, the idea of Norman was birthed. The beginning was jokes about Norman, the Farting Elephant, which was renamed Norman PhartEphant®.

As their household expanded to include two beautiful boys, the timing seemed right to release the idea of Norman PhartEphant® on the unsuspecting public.

Norman PhartEphant® has transcended from an idea, to a plush toy, to a story of adoption, transition, and overcoming odds.

Fierce Fun Toys, LLC is a philanthropic, yet for profit, company with a portion of our proceeds supporting children's charities. To read more on the charities - Half the Sky (supporting orphans in China) and The Smile Train (helping children with cleft lip/palette worldwide), please visit www.FierceFunToys.com.

We know we can't help everyone,
but that shouldn't stop us from trying to help someone.